The Steeple People

The Snow Circus

Bobby Days

About the Author

Bobby Days has lived in Combe and the neighbouring village, Stonesfield, all his life, which is where most of the adventures of the Steeple People are set. Bobby has also spent a great deal of time in Cornwall over the years and has built strong relationships in the small seaside town of Mousehole where some of the characters visit from time to time in the series. He has been a Stonesfield Slate Roofer for 35 years and is the main roofer for Blenheim Palace Estates: another setting for our intrepid adventurers! He has had the idea for these novels since his daughter, Shelley, was born in 1990 and finally got round to writing about the adventures of the Steeple People in 2012.

The Steeple People – the Snow Circus, is the first in a trilogy of novels about the steeple people family.

The right of Bobby Days to be identified as the author of the work has been asserted by him in accordance with the Copyright, Designs and Patents Act 1988.

ISBN 978-1519289384
third edition

Cover Illustration by Nina Truman

Printed for Bobby Days in Great Britain by
CreateSpace

Thank you

There are many people to thank for their support and encouragement to get the story of The Steeple People told but a few special mentions;

To Shelley, my beautiful daughter of whom I am so proud who inspired me to write this story.
Lynda and Andrew, for the final push
Nina, for your fantastic illustrations.
Lee and Elena, Moray and Rosie, and Annette Rainbow.

And finally to Vikki, who without her belief in me and all her hard work, this would never have been possible.

Chapter One

This is a story about some wonderful little people who dwell in the top of the steeple, overlooking the front of Chatterpie Grange in Combelonga, in the Wolds. A long time ago some people chose to live in houses like you and me. Others chose to live underground in the old disused gold mines and they are known as Fizzlers.

And those who made their home in the steeples of the land, were of course known as Steeple People.

This is Lulu's story.

Lulu's father is called Jack and her mother is known as Mam. They've lived in the steeple all their lives, in fact their family has lived there for generations. Lulu has two brothers, Tiff (short for Christopher) and Joey. She also has a sister named Shellsbells. They all live with their cousins, the brothers, Buster, Bumble and Bob.

 Over the years they have adapted to living in steeple-sized spaces so they are little people about 30 cm tall.

Usually, we can't actually see or hear them but if there's a thunderstorm and the sky is full of electricity you might get a glimpse of them. It's like looking into a river and suddenly you spot a fish, but in a moment it's gone and you wonder if you really did see it or not.

The Steeple People can also do magic. They can shrink things to 'minify' them or 'maxify' them to make them bigger. They do this by holding their noses, pinching their ears, and crossing their legs whilst whistling. It all looks very funny but it works.

Jack works mostly on the roof cleaning all the gutters and repairing slipped slates, which keeps the whole of The Grange nice and dry. Mam keeps the steeple looking spick and span and cares for the family, cooking wonderful meals for them all.

This story begins on a cold, blustery day, near lunchtime. The first flakes of snow floated down past the stained glass of the kitchen window. It was the Christmas holidays and both girls were helping their mum to prepare lunch.

Lulu was the first to notice the snow and rushed over to the steamed up window to have a closer look, as she went, she accidently knocked over a bowl of eggs. Turning quickly she leapt back and caught it just before it hit the floor, but in doing so, her foot stamped on Shell's big toe.

"Owww!" Cried Shell, jumping back and grabbing hold of the table to steady herself. "Lu, that hurt."

"Sorry Shell. I didn't mean to. I just got so excited about the snow," she placed the bowl of eggs back on the table carefully, unbelievably none of them had broken. Peering out of the window she could see the snow had already started to settle. Turning round to her mum she asked, "What's the weather got be like before the Snow Circus can come?"

"Well," she replied thoughtfully, "The wind would have to be coming from the north-northeast and the temperature would need to go down to minus 10 degrees."

"That's cold," Lulu said, pretending to shiver.

Pressing her nose against the window and making circles in the steam with her finger she asked, "If the circus does come will the King and Queen of Snowland come too?"

"As far as I recall I think it's been over a fifty years since they've come," her mother replied, drying her hands on her apron.

"Fifty years! Blimey, that's a long time. I wonder why?"

"Oh, they're very busy darling. They visit other lands, which takes up a lot of their time and also the weather conditions have to be just right for them to get here. So if it carries on snowing like this and the temperature drops, then there is a good chance the circus will come, but I wouldn't know about the King and Queen. Now girls, let's clear the rest of the dishes away and when you're finished you can check the weather vane on top of the steeple to see if the cockerel is pointing north-northeast."

Lulu smiled and tingled with excitement at the thought of all the wonderful things that could happen if The Snow Circus came.

Chapter Two

After Lulu had finished helping her mum, she raced up the steps inside the steeple two at a time to get to the very top. She had a good view of the weathervane through a small leaded window. The snow was now swirling around and the clouds were as dark and heavy as lead. Lulu squealed with delight, the weathervane was, in fact, facing north-northeast and shining brightly in the dark afternoon sky.

She bounded back down the stairs, through the kitchen and along the corridor leading to the living room, where her dad had just taken off his boots to warm his feet in front of the roaring log fire.

Tiff and Joey sat at the table, playing a game of battleships, while Shellsbells was doing some needlepoint. Bumble, Buster and Bob were sitting around the fire, lounging on some very comfortable chairs, after they'd just come in from stocking up the firewood.

Everyone was looking forward to their lunch when suddenly the door burst open and Lulu hurtled in shouting, "It's SNOWING."

"Blimey," said Tiff, "You quite frit us Lu, you did."

"Snowing?" they all said together. Jack got up to look out of the window to see for himself. There was a thin layer of snow covering the roofs and tower already. He turned to the boys,

"We'd better have our lunch sharpish lads, so we can get out there to get the tree and the last of the Christmas provisions. If it's coming on like this we could be snowed in for ages."

After a very satisfying lunch, and with full tummies, they set off out into the cold.

"I'll put the spiked tyres on the motorbike," said Jack. "Buster, call up the pheasant and the partridges so you can get the groceries we need from the mill please. I'll get the Christmas tree."

"Of course, Jack," Buster replied.

Putting his fingers in his mouth he gave two sharp whistles followed by one long one to call the birds. The sound was muffled by the wind and the snow, so he had to whistle again.

By the time Jack got the tyres on his motorbike, the birds had arrived. Bumble and Bob harnessed the partridges and Buster saddled up the pheasant. Leaping on the birds they were ready to go.

Pheasants and partridges live in the woods and the fields. Many years ago, Jack managed to save these birds from the Poachers who were trying to catch them to eat. The birds never forgot Jack's kindness and became very fond of him and the family, letting them stroke their feathers and eventually letting them ride on their backs. A sort of thank you, you could say. In return, Jack fed them and made sure they were safe, not just from the Poachers but also from other wild creatures.

Pheasants are amazing. They can take off almost vertically but partridges need a long run up to take off. Once they were all up in the air they turned South and started flying towards the old watermill.

Putting on his hat, goggles and gloves, Jack was ready to go too, and so was Lulu, who had pleaded with her dad to let her ride with him on the back of his motorbike. Jack strapped Lulu tightly on and jumped on himself and started it up.

Lulu had put on her thickest, furriest, warmest coat and bobble hat, with yellow goggles covering her eyes. They were now ready to go and fetch the Christmas tree.

Mam was waving her apron out of the steeple window to say good-bye.

Jack caught a glimpse of her and smiled. He loved her so much and the thought of the lovely warm fire and all the smells of the spices from the delicious food they would come home to later, made him very happy.

Waving back to her, he turned the motorbike around and off they went. Slowly at first, because it was very slippery but gathering speed gradually, they headed off through the snowy fields. The cold wind was biting at their faces and their hands were growing numb but they were exhilarated by the power of the motorbike and a real sense of adventure.

Chapter Three

Buster, Bumble and Bob were heading down the river towards the mill and were skimming the water, flying in a V formation so those pesky Poachers would find them harder to detect. The Poachers were often out to bag a pheasant or two, trying to catch them in their aerial nets or shoot them to cook for their supper. The boys had to fly very fast and low, which was extremely difficult through the snow and swirling wind. Keeping their heads down, they went as fast as the birds could fly.

Jack and Lulu were going the other way, up to the woods where the Christmas trees grew. The snow was laying thickly on the ground now, a full two and a half centimetres, which doesn't seem much to us, but to Jack and Lulu it was over their wellies.

"Hold on tight," Jack called over his shoulder.

Lulu could hardly hear him above the roar of the engine and the wind, but she knew what he meant. Jack changed gear and throttled hard up the hill making the back wheel spin and spray snow everywhere.

Meanwhile, still flying in a V formation, Buster signalled to Bob and Bumble, pointing towards the watermill in the distance.

"Only another quarter of a mile," he called but his words were lost in the wind. They knew it wasn't far because they could see the lights of the mill in the distance. The snow kept sticking to their goggles so they had to keep clearing their lenses with their mittens.

It was a real nuisance but they carried on regardless.

Jack and Lulu had reached the edge of the wood. It was growing dark, so Jack put the bike on its stand and left the engine running with the lights on full beam. Jumping off and wading through the snow to the smallest tree, he started to climb it, having spotted that the top had been damaged and was lying at an odd angle. It would only need a short, sharp tug for it to come down. It would be perfect for them.

With the rope looped round his shoulder he quickly climbed to the top. Tying the rope around the very tip of the tree he climbed down the branches, keeping one end of the rope in his hand he jumped and landed in the soft snow with a crumping sound.

Shaking his head and removing his hat to clear the snow from his ears, he winked at Lulu. Smiling back she gave him the thumbs up. Tying the rope to the motorbike, he jumped back on, turned it around and very gently drove it down the hill until the rope became taut. Slowly it started to pull the top of the tree towards the ground.

They heard a loud crack as the top broke off completely and fell to the ground. Immediately it started to bounce and rolled down towards them, and as it did, it gathered speed and snow, getting bigger and bigger. Jack had to do something quickly, so he yanked hard at the loose end of the slipknot attached to the back of the bike. Turning around sharply, he accelerated out of the way. They watched the big ball of snow-covered tree roll right past them, luckily it came to a stop not far from them when it hit a large rock which knocked off most of the snow.

'Phew, that was close', thought Jack. He cleared his goggles and picked up the rope, using it to attach the tree to the back of the bike.

"We best be on our way home before the snow gets any deeper," he shouted over the howling wind.

Lulu nodded and gave him another thumbs up. Jack turned the bike towards home and they started to make their way through the blizzard back towards home.

The others had arrived at the mill and were circling, looking for a good place to land. Once they had located a good spot from the air, they leaned back on the birds and they began to descend. Nearing the ground the birds also leaned back with their legs pointing out and started using their wings as brakes by flapping hard, and gently one by one, landed in the powdery white snow. The boys jumped off and leading the birds by the reins, secured them to a log and gave them a handful of corn.

Making their way through the snow, they went over a drawbridge to the small red door of the mill, next to the big water wheel. They stomped their boots on the mat to loosen the snow then Buster pulled the handle of a chain hanging by the side of the door. In the distance they could hear the sound of a bell ringing, and then they heard someone walking towards them with heavy, clumping steps. They waited patiently.

"Who's there?" called a gruff voice from behind the door.
"It's the Steeplers," replied Bumble with a slight tremble in his voice.
"We've come for our Christmas hamper, please, sir." The three boys

saw a small panel on the door slowly open and a face appeared.

"You're late! I'm just shutting up shop," and with that he slammed the panel firmly shut then opened the big, creaky door. Scowling at them he said "Come on in then, and wipe yer feet, 'urry Up!"

The man, Mr Pumphery, was plump with a bright red round face. He was wearing a squat-brimmed hat with a blue ribbon round it. His waistcoat was yellow and he wore it under a blue short tailored coat with plus four trousers (plus four means they stop four inches below the knee). His socks were the same bright yellow as his waistcoat. On his feet were big, black hobnailed boots. Hobnails are rounded metal studs set into the sole of the boot to make them grip in the mud. They are quite fun to see at night, if you scuff them across a stone path, they will spark.

Walking after the brightly-clothed man through the darkness, there was a strong, heady smell of flour, treacle and dried fruit, and other wonderful spices. As their eyes became accustomed to the dark they could make out the shapes of sacks of flour and boxes of all kinds of interesting things bought from the sailors who came down the river.

Mr Pumphrey was from a different family who had decided to live on the ground and settle in the mill. They've lived there for many years ago in one of the small rooms near the big water wheel.

Mr Pumphrey turned round and pointed with a plump finger to a crate in the corner of the room.

"Your groceries are over there so you'd better get a move on. I'm closing up soon, my wife has got my tea ready and I don't want it to get cold."

"Okay," replied Buster, "we'll have it all out of here in a jiffy. Come on, lads, let's put our backs into it."

Christmas came in a large box. Now they had to push it outside on rollers, connect it up to the harness under the pheasant, pay Mr Pumphrey, and get off home as quickly as they could. As Bumble put his hat and gloves back on, he spotted a sign over another little door. *Rocket Shop* it read in big yellow letters.

'So that's where they get the fireworks for New Year and bonfire night', he thought. He made his way over to take a look. Rubbing the glass windowpane with his mitten he peered through to see the window display.

"Wow," he sighed. What a brilliant sight. There were multi-coloured rockets of all sizes, some no bigger than a pen, some the size of a man, and all had different names printed down the side of them: cloud-buster, meteor-storm, and thunder-strike. What fantastic names he thought. There were big round Catherine wheels; jumping jacks (these are a lot of bangers tied together on a fuse so that when one went off, it lit another and then that went off, about twenty times, ever so quick, like a quick-fire machine gun, bang, bang, bang bang). Roman candles called Mount Vesuvius, little demons, cannons, sparklers, jack-in-the-boxes and aeroplanes, to name just a few.

Bumble filled with joy at the thought of them all going off in a fantastic display of colour and noise. Turning back to Buster and Bob he gave a low whistle, "Can't wait for the next bonfire night, lads."

It was now very dark and the wind had got up again. Luckily it was blowing the same way as they were going, which would help a great deal on their dangerous flight back. After quite a few hard flaps of its wings the pheasant took off vertically with the box hanging below. Buster turned the light on his helmet onto full beam and Bob did the same. Bumble and Bob jumped onto their partridges and took off, following Buster into the freezing cold night.

Jack and Lulu were nearly home now and they could see the lights of the Grange getting nearer, a lovely, orange glow shone through the windows. Lulu's nose was blue with the cold and Jack's fingers were freezing as they battled against the wind and snow. Jack squeezed Lulu's knee to reassure her and she smiled again.

"Not far now sweetheart," he mouthed as they turned the last bend up towards the drawbridge.

They had only completed the drawbridge in the autumn for bonfire night, so they could wheel out all the fireworks in one go and if it rained they could quickly get them back in again, but that's another story.

Tiff, Joey and Shells, were waiting patiently in the steeple for Jack and Lulu's return. They were watching the small pinprick of light gently snaking its way back towards them. As the motorbike approached, they jumped onto the fireman's pole that ran from the steeple to the ground. One at a time they slid down and were on the ground within seconds. Tiff yanked on the chains and the drawbridge lowered.

"Well done," shouted Jack as he and Lulu drove through.

Both boys saluted them and jumped and clapped their hands together.

"WOW, that's a fine tree." Joey exclaimed. "It will look fabulous with all the decorations and lights on it."

"Bagsy I put the baubles on," Shells said as she felt the pine needles on one of the branches.

"And I'll put the lights on," said Tiff, poking Joe in the ribs with his elbow.

"Where are the lads, aren't they back yet?" asked Jack, looking concerned.

They all turned to look back along the river to see if there was any sign of Buster, Bob and Bumble but all they could see was swirling snow, against a pitch black sky.

Chapter Four

Buster, Bob and Bumble were flying back as fast as the wind could carry them, almost touching the water at times. Buster turned his head to see if Bumble and Bob were okay but as he turned back he caught a glimpse of light in the corner of his eye.

"Up," he shouted to them, "Up quick!"

Within a second all three of them were rocketing up in the air. There was an almighty bang and a flash of yellow light in front of them.

Buster banked left and Bumble swerved to the right. Bob was also turning when he suddenly shrieked out in pain and put his hand up to his ear.

"Aaaarrgghhh! Something just hit me," he squealed. Bumble looked down and could just make out the dark silhouettes of two men pointing shotguns at them.

"Bank to the left, lads," Bumble cried, "and drop down low, quickly, or else they'll get us." Down they went, almost into the river. They heard another crack of gunfire. There was an amazing whizzing and whistling sound flying past their heads, but this time everybody was okay. The Poachers had taken another shot but, thankfully, missed. Of course, you will realise that all the Poachers could see were the birds, because the Steeplers were invisible to them.

On and on the lads went, flying low for another five minutes, skimming the water, until they saw the glimmer of lights of The Grange ahead of them. The birds were very tired by now but were still flapping as hard as they could.

All of them were frozen and couldn't wait to get safely indoors.

"My goodness," Bumble whispered to himself, "I thought we'd had it that time."

Joey, looking through the leaded window of the steeple, spotted them coming round the bend of the river, their three little lights bobbing up and down in the distance.

"There they are Dad, they're coming." he shouted, whilst pointing in their direction.

The three birds landed together, in the deep snow. Bumble was off first and ran straight over to Bob, who was still clutching his ear.

"Are you alright mate?" he was very worried.

"Ah, it's just a nick," Bob replied. "Those pesky Poachers nearly had us that time. I'm lucky to have escaped with just a graze."

It took twenty minutes to unload the crate and stack it away inside. Tiff was wheeling the wheelbarrow and Joey the sack truck while Buster and the others were giving the pheasant and partridges some well-deserved corn and a vigorous rub down to warm them up.

Lulu looked over to Buster. "Didn't they do a brilliant job?" she said while stroking the pheasants neck.

"They certainly did," he agreed. "Better just check they're okay, they had a close shave out there."

Buster ran his hands down the feathers of each bird, just to make sure.

"Yep, they seem alright, just a few feathers missing. They can roost up in the loft tonight to keep warm out of this blizzard."

He climbed the steps to the loft with the birds hopping up the steps after him. After lighting the lanterns, the birds tucked into their food and water then settled for the night on the freshly laid straw.

Chapter Five

Everyone was now inside and the drawbridge was pulled up tight to keep out wandering animals and to stop the wind and snow blowing in. The birds were all tucked up in the loft. All was well.

It was a long way up to the rooms in the steeple, four flights of stairs in fact, so to make it easier to go up, Jack had built a lift system, which worked very well. He'd made two wooden crates (about the size of shoeboxes to you and me) and fixed a pulley wheel right at the top of the steeple. He had tied a rope to the top of one of the crates, threaded the rope up and over the pulley wheel then down to the top of the other one. Both the crates were at ground level, but one was over the trapdoor into the cellars, so when anybody wanted to go up, someone heavier got in the crate over the trapdoor, pulled the lever, which opened the door and down it went, lifting the other crate up.

Bumble and Buster stepped into the first crate and the rest packed the other one with the Christmas goodies. Bumble pulled the lever and up went the other crate and down went theirs – simple. Of course, it worked the other way round if they wanted anything from the cellars to be brought up.

Once everything had been packed away it was teatime so they all sat around the table. Shells brought out the pies and sausage rolls while Mam put a plaster on poor old Bob's ear. She was very gentle with him because it was very sore. She then put a bandage around the top of his head to keep the plaster in place, knowing he'd keep picking at it and making it worse if she didn't. When she'd finished he went and sat down at the table with everyone else. Tiff and Joey nudged each other under the table, trying not to laugh at him, because he looked so comical.

"Well everyone, I think we've got enough of everything to have a great Christmas, so let's not dally," said Jack. "When we've finished our tea we'll get cracking and put up the decorations."

"I've already called bagsy on putting the baubles on the tree, Dad," said Shells.

"Well done love, so if you like lads, you can put up the fairy lights."

"After you've all washed up," added Mam. "Then you can decorate the whole room with streamers, paper chains, tinsel, and Chinese lanterns."

They all had great fun putting the decorations up right around the room, blowing up balloons, hanging the lights around the picture rail and dressing the tree.

When they'd finished it was nearly bedtime.

"Tomorrow's Christmas Eve," yawned Buster and they all nodded in agreement smiling at each other.

"Can't wait!" said Tiff, also yawning.

"Nor can I," echoed the girls together and suddenly they were all giggles and excitement.

"Turn out the main light then, Buster, let's get in the mood." Mam's eyes twinkled with anticipation.

"Three... two...one," they all counted down. "Wow," they all chorused, as the fairy lights went on and the main light went out, "what a lovely sight."

The tree was a kaleidoscope of twinkling colours, festooned in tinsel and sparkling baubles and with the fire crackling in the hearth, it was perfect.

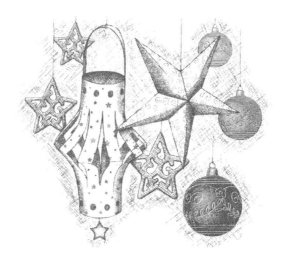

Jack, Buster, Bob and Bumble sat down around the fireside whilst the girls brought them some Christmas cheer in the form of home-made elderberry wine and strawberry juice, which they'd made the year before.

It was nearly midnight when a tired Jack finally went to bed, after turning all the lights off and making sure the fire was safe.

Lulu was in bed, looking out through the gap in the curtains at the still falling snow. Smiling to herself because this really was still her favourite time of year, and if the Snow Circus came it would be the best ever. Turning over, she turned out the light and settled down to sleep.

Chapter Six

It was a snowy Christmas Eve morning. The wind had whipped up the snow into long drifts across the fields. In some places it must have been at least fifteen centimetres deep on the ground but the drifts were almost three times that.

Lulu woke to the sound of her dad poking the embers from last night's fire. Rubbing her eyes she yawned and stretched then drawing back the curtains, she saw the panes of glass were frozen on the inside as well as out. She scraped the ice off and looked out at the magical scene outside. It was total whiteness everywhere, except for some trees standing out, like upside down witches' brooms.

In the field below she noticed some movement, it was Joey and Tiff having a snowball fight, wearing brightly coloured hats and scarves, they were darting wildly about. They had built two snowmen, facing each other, with arms outstretched, shaking hands. 'Now that's clever', she thought.

She dressed quickly because she wanted to join the fun before breakfast.

Pulling on her hat and coat, and wrapping herself in her scarf, she ran out into the snow. It was so cold it took her breath away but she didn't mind because it was so exhilarating to be out there with her brothers and sister.

"Let's build an igloo," shouted Shellsbells through her cupped hands.
"Great idea," agreed Tiff.

So they ran indoors and collected some shovels and buckets.
It took them ages to build, but once they had finished the outside they turned their attention to the inside and hollowed out holes for seats and more holes in the walls for candle holders.

It was lunchtime by the time they'd finished and they had all built up quite an appetite, so when they heard their mother calling they were really pleased. They quickly covered the igloo with snow and packed it down hard with their hands.

Collecting up all the tools they took them back to the steeple, running up the stairs to the kitchen for lunch.

Chapter Seven

The family were sitting in front of the roaring fire after their meal when they heard a commotion outside. Shells got up and went to the window to take a look. The sound was coming from the front of The Grange, or, as they sometimes called it, "The Big House".

A carriage and four white horses had just pulled up in the courtyard, at the front door. The driver jumped down and opened the door and a very pretty lady stepped down. Her dress was a beautiful turquoise and her hat had a long peacock feather attached to one side of it. A gentleman got out next, wearing a top hat and tails.

Jack walked over to the window and put his hand gently on Shells' shoulder, whispering in her ear. "They must be coming to stay at the Big House, in time for the Christmas Ball this evening. Shall we go and have a look later?"

"Now then, Jack, I heard that. You know what happened the last time you went and had a look," Mam chuckled, seeing the naughtiness in his eyes.

"I ended up having to take your boots off when you got back after all the elderberry wine you drank. You know the big-un's wine is much stronger than ours."

"Oh Mum, we'll be there to keep an eye on him tonight. The last time we weren't old enough to go with them," Shellsbells pleaded.

"Hmm, well. If you do go, make sure you stay out of sight. Bumble nearly got spotted last time, fooling about, pretending to be a cockerel, strutting around, flapping his arms like a mad thing. One of the guests nearly stepped on him when he was doing the foxtrot. The fact that he managed to slip under the bottom of the sofa out of the way was pure luck," said Mam.

"Pure genius you mean," muttered Bumble smiling to himself.

"Okay Mam," replied Jack, "we'll be extra careful." There was a twinkle in his eye as he shot a sideways glance at Shells. He has a big, cheesy grin on his face.

Chapter Eight

The children were on their way down the stairs to go back outside when they heard their mum call out, "Don't be late back, it's our special Christmas Eve tea at 4 o'clock, then you're all going up to the Big House afterwards to see the ball."

"Okay," they called back, grabbing some blankets and some home-made candles from the cupboard. Making their way to the igloo, each one of them saluted the snowmen as they passed under their outstretched arms. Once inside they arranged the blankets on the seats and placed the candles into the holes they had made in the walls, and then lit them with a match making it lovely and cosy.

"Gosh, this is going to be the best Christmas ever," said Lulu. "What with the ball tonight, Christmas Day tomorrow and maybe the Snow Circus."

Shells nodded and giggled in agreement, she was so excited.

The boys played cards and the girls sang carols whilst making Christmas cards for their parents.

It was no time at all before they heard a distant whistle. Joey shuffled through the tunnel of the igloo and looked out. It was getting quite dark now and all the lights were starting to twinkle in the big house. Flaming torches had been lit around the courtyard and down the stream leading to the lake, which was twinkling from the reflections of all the lights. Huge spotlights shone up from the ground onto the walls of the house, making it a lovely orangey colour, so warm and inviting against the bitter cold late afternoon.

"Mum's calling us for tea, everyone, let's get going. We don't want to be late," said Joey.

With that they all bundled out of the igloo and ran up the path to the drawbridge, taking the stairs two at a time until they reached the dining room. They were all panting hard by the time they got there.

What a spread they had! Delicious pies; a whole baked ham; fresh bread; pickles; cakes and a large trifle. It was a picture with them all sitting there, having pulled their Christmas crackers and wearing colourful paper hats, especially Bob with his bandaged head and his hat perched on top at a funny angle.

"Well Mam, you've done us proud yet again," said Jack. "Let's raise a glass to her everyone. God bless you, Mam," they cried and they all clinked their glasses together with a resounding, "Cheers!"

Chapter Nine

Chatterpie Grange is in an L shape, with the back of the house facing the lake, and the front and side facing the driveway and fountain. The steeple is on the turret of the tower, and from it you can look down onto the front door and up the driveway to the big arched gateway. The steeple and turret are connected to the big house. There is a series of underground rooms, all connected by a tunnel which leads into the basement below the kitchen and into a store room under the grand hall.

Jack held the lantern up in the air so those following could see where they were going. The glow cast long shadows behind him. They'd been walking along the passage between the turret and the kitchen towards the grand hall for about fifteen minutes. Making their way through the winding underground passage, they had to crawl down the slopes on their hands and knees and jump over puddles to get to the room directly under the grand hall. Buster had bumped his head at least three times on the way through and Bumble had ripped his new coat on a nail sticking out of a wooden beam.

Jack put his fingers to his lips telling them to be quiet. They could feel the music vibrating through the walls and floor, above them they could hear people laughing.

"Right," Jack whispered, "the ladders are leaning against the wall over there, we'll move them over to the trapdoor". Bumble and Tiff carried them over and carefully placed them in position.

"I'm going up first," declared Jack. "Bumble, you stand at the bottom of the ladder to steady me."

Jack started to climb and Bumble stood at the base of the ladder with his foot on the bottom rung. When Jack got to the top he pushed with his head under the trapdoor and it moved up a bit. He pushed again, this time with his hands and it went up just enough for him to see into the room. He gave a long, low whistle, the sight that greeted him was quite wonderful. A mouth-watering aroma of roast beef and Yorkshire pudding wafted through the small gap of the opened trapdoor, straight up his nose. As the warm air hit him he nearly lost his grip on the top of the ladder.

The trapdoor was in the corner of the grand hall, against the wall. A table laden with food and drink was above it, a tablecloth was draped over it, almost touching the floor. It was a beautiful red and gold material, with piping around the edge and tassels that dangled down at each corner. Looking out from under the cloth Jack could see everything in the room but nobody could see him. He looked around at the sparkling candelabras, lit with what seemed like hundreds of candles. He could see beautiful sculptures and paintings and the whole room was decorated with holly, ivy, paper chains, and fairy lights.

A huge Christmas tree, decorated with lights and with presents around it, stood in the opposite corner. There was a large marble fireplace piled high with burning logs, with flames leaping up the chimney, sparks crackling as they went.

Everybody was dressed in their best clothes for the ball; fabulous ball gowns for the ladies and smart black dinner jackets with bow ties for the gentlemen. Everyone was smiling, laughing and talking. The tables were laden with a wonderful buffet of lobsters, seafood platters, cheeses, savoury pies and meats of every description. Towards the end of the table was a huge trifle and a selection of cakes.

The band was on the stage to the left, playing a lively jig. There must have been about forty people dancing. The rest were sitting or standing by, enjoying themselves, drinking and eating. Jack looked back down into the cellar and whispered, "Right, up you come one at a time and I'll pull you through the trapdoor."

When they were all up, Bumble decided to go and find some snacks, he always had an insatiable appetite.

Buster followed him, lifting up the tablecloths every now and then as he went. As they sidled around the skirting board, Bumble spotted a hamper and a bottle of wine through a slightly opened door. He turned to Buster and gestured to him to look. Buster came up behind him and Bumble spoke quietly into his ear.

"Shall we go and see if it's going spare?" He winked.

"If you mean steal it, I'll box your ears," whispered Buster, crossly.

"No, no, I didn't mean that at all. Sometimes they have hampers for the people of the village that they give out on Christmas morning, this could be one of those," said Bumble, looking hurt.

Now the music was playing loud and fast and everybody was dancing in a large circle in the middle of the room, going round and round. Bumble and Buster saw their chance and made a dash to the open door.

Jack, Shells, and Lulu were lying down on their tummies, looking out, from underneath the tablecloth, at the spectacle in the room.

"Wouldn't it be wonderful to dance like that, Dad?" said Shells, dreamily.

"Did you know Aunt Lucy was a dancer?" replied Jack, pausing for a moment, he added, "She's moved to a lovely little tower on a pier in Cornwall. If you like I'll get in touch with her and see if you can stay for a couple of weeks in the summer next year. Maybe she'll teach you to dance."

"Oh thanks, Dad, that would be great."

"Can I go too, Dad?" asked Lulu.

"Of course you can love," he replied. "It'll be great fun. You can go on the train."

Meanwhile, Bumble and Buster shut the door with their backs, then crept over to the hamper. Once their eyes had adjusted to the dimmer light, they inspected the contents; there were lots of lovely things in there including a silver bottle with a small gold chain around its neck. Attached to it was a label. Bumble stood on his tiptoes to have a closer look. To his surprise, in beautiful italic writing there was a message.

"To the little people we know dwell here
Enjoy this fare for your good cheer.
Dance and jig to your delight.
Come and join us on this Christmas Eve night."

"Blimey." exclaimed Bumble. "Buster come over here and have a look at this."

"Flippin 'eck, they know we're here! Do you think they can see us?"

"No way. Never. We're too careful to let that happen." said Bumble, almost falling over his words.

"Well they must do or else they wouldn't have gone to all this trouble," replied Buster.

Bumble thought carefully for a moment, scratching his head, then said very quietly, "I reckon it's a trap. They want us to take this as bait and when we do, they'll chuck a net over us and catch us. Then they'll show us off, just like pets."

"Don't be so stupid!" Buster grabbed Bumble's arm and spun him round. "I don't think they would, you know. They are much too kind. Anyway, forget about that, we're wasting time, we should minify the goodies and take them back to the rest of the gang."

So, with that, they held their noses, pinched their ears, crossed their legs, and whistled, whilst holding on to the hamper. Within a flash the bottle and the hamper shrank to Steeple People size. Bumble put the bottle in his pocket and Buster put the hamper under his arm. Opening the door slowly, and after checking it was all clear, they ran as fast as they could back towards the trapdoor.

It was not fast enough though. Just as they were approaching the tablecloth, Mungo, the highland terrier, who had been snoozing in front of the fire, spotted them out of the corner of his eye. Within a second he was pelting across the dance floor straight after them, skidding as he ran on the polished floor.

"Run, Bumble." shouted Buster. "Run for your life, the dog, the dog, it's after us."

Mungo was right behind them and gaining fast.

"Jack. Jack." shouted Buster "Get everybody below."

But Jack had already spotted what was going on and had sent the rest of them scurrying through the opening of the trapdoor and back down the ladder.

"Hurry!" Jack called.

Looking behind him, Bumble saw the dog was very close. Buster was the first to jump, followed by Bumble, who, clearing the side of the trapdoor by centimetres, landed on an old mattress Tiff and Joey had just dragged over and placed directly under the trapdoor.

BOING! Bumble bounced as he landed and as he did the bottle flew out of his jacket pocket and straight up in the air. Diving for it, Bob caught it with both hands, landing on his back on the mattress. Luckily, Buster had landed on his feet, arms wrapped around the hamper.

Jack slammed the trapdoor shut just as the dog's nose brushed up against it. "Phew, that was another close shave," he gasped looking down. "Well, everyone, I think that's enough excitement for one night. Shall we make our way home?"

They all looked at each other and nodded in agreement. Buster and Bumble were still panting after their ordeal, but the rest of them were very pleased at what they had got and were looking forward to investigating the contents of the hamper.

"What a stroke of luck finding that, Bumble," exclaimed Jack, whilst inspecting the hamper.
"Just like we were meant to," Bumble grinned.

Chapter Ten

It didn't take as long to get back to the steeple as it did getting to the grand hall. Isn't it funny, a journey home never takes as long?

All they could talk about, as they walked back, was the label on the bottle and finding the hamper, and as the whole story was told over and over again, it became more elaborate with each telling but they still couldn't fathom it out. Buster and Bumble gave the hamper and the bottle to Jack as they got in the lift.

"See you up top then lads," Jack said pulling the lever, letting them go down as the rest of them went up.

It was about fifteen minutes before Bumble and Buster appeared in the warm living room of the steeple after their long climb up the stairs.

"Open the hamper, then, Joey," said Bob, rummaging around trying to find a bottle opener.

"Okay then," he replied, undoing the buckles of the two leather straps securing the lid to the wicker basket. Lifting the lid fully open, they all looked in and stared in wonderment. There were biscuits, jams, pâtés, cakes, rolls, crisps, chocolates, bubble-gum and sherbet dip-dabs.

"Come on, Mam, get some plates and glasses out, we'll have a party up here instead and a jolly good old knees-up," announced Jack cheerfully. When they had finished eating all the goodies, Lulu put some Christmas music on. The boys moved the table and chairs to one side and they had a dance round and round the living room. Each one of them put a hand in the middle making a star whilst going around in a circle.

And that's how Christmas Eve ended, the fire glowing in the hearth, the fairy lights twinkling on the tree and the snow gently falling outside. Everybody was tired but happy and ready for bed.

Lulu was the first to go. "Goodnight everyone, I'm off now," she said putting her hand to her mouth stifling a big yawn.

"Don't forget to hang up your stocking, sweetheart, Old Santa will be coming tonight, if he can get through the blizzard." Mam said

"Oh, I do hope so." Lulu answered as she blew everyone a kiss good night before making her way to her room.

Lying in bed, she went over in her mind the events of the evening and what might happen tomorrow. Lying there, lost in her own thoughts, she was suddenly brought back to the present by a faint sound of jingle bells ringing in the distance.

Jumping out of bed and going over to the window, she drew back the curtains and started scraping the ice off the windowpane.

"Is it? Is it?" she whispered to herself, hoping that it was the sound of the snow circus arriving.

Looking through the frozen glass, past the swirling snowflakes towards the Big House, she could see all the guests from the party had gathered on the south terrace, the ladies were wrapped in warm coats and hats, and the gentlemen in smart scarves and gloves.

Whoosh! A firework soared high into the sky and exploded into a brilliant red heart shape, then another rocket flew up in the shape of an arrow, straight through the big red heart. Three more fireworks exploded next to each other, shooting out stars like glass chandeliers sparkling and then falling down slowly into the wind. For the finale, a series of fireworks flew up and went off, each in the shape of a letter, and when they had finished, *MERRY CHRISTMAS* was spelt out in red, green, silver, and gold.

"Wow," Lulu sighed. As the last of the sparkles floated away she could just hear all the ladies and gentlemen wishing each other "Merry Christmas."

She heard the tinkling of bells again and saw a dozen carriages were forming a semicircle, lining up, to take the guests home. Each carriage had six lanterns, two white, two orange, and two red at the back. Dazzling white horses attached to the ornate carriages were nodding their heads and stamping their hooves in the snow. Their manes were plaited with red and gold ribbons with little sleigh bells woven in.

'How beautiful', she thought.

She watched as the carriages began to fill up with guests and proceed up the drive, jingling as they went. Lulu was tired now and yawned as the last carriage disappeared into the night. Watching the torches go out one by one, she slowly pulled the curtains closed, tip-toed back to her bed, cuddled her hot water bottle, and closed her eyes. She drifted off into a lovely, warm slumber full of dreams of ladies in fabulous dresses and fireworks lighting up the snowy night sky.

Chapter Eleven

"Merry Christmas, everybody," was the first thing Lulu heard that Christmas morning. It took her a moment or two to wake up and open her eyes, and then to realise what day it was.

"Christmas? It's Christmas. Yee-hah!" Throwing back the blankets she dashed over to the window but all she could see was snow, snow and more snow.

Sighing to herself she felt a bit disappointed. 'No circus yet but maybe tonight it will come', she thought.

Returning to her bed she saw that her stocking was brimming over with presents.

She was super thrilled when she saw that two of the presents were ski-shaped. That was perfect because hers were getting too small for her. Ripping open the wrapping paper she pulled them out, they were all shiny and new. There was a knock at her door and Shells came in excitedly saying, "Merry Christmas, Lu."

"And the same to you, sis."

"Wow, you've got a set of skis too," said Shells.

"Yep, and they look a bit special to me," she replied happily.

"What do you mean?"

"Well, look at the back of them, they've got fins. You don't have fins on ordinary skis, do you?" she replied.

"No, you're right," said Jack, as he entered the room with two steaming mugs of hot chocolate. "Them is very special skis," placing the mugs on the table, he explained. "They've been made especially for you in Santa's workshop and they have magical qualities. It says so on the label. Look."

To make these hover skis perform,
Just tap the front of each one with your ski poles.
As you start to move, lean forward and jump – batteries not included.

"Does that mean we can fly in them, Dad?" Shells asked.

"Well, it looks like it to me, girls. Now drink up your chocolate and get dressed, then you can come to the living room and we'll open the rest of our presents together."

Everyone else had been very busy since daybreak. Mam had been the first up. In the living room, she'd picked up all the tinsel and baubles from the floor, knocked off the tree by Bumble the night before, after he'd tripped over the box of crackers and fell into it, sending the decorations everywhere. Unfortunately, while trying to free himself, he'd managed to get the fairy-lights tangled around his legs, fell over again, onto the table this time knocking the bowl of trifle flying into the air. Unfortunately, it had landed upside down on his head. As he had lifted it off, the custard had run down his face and out of his ears, and the jelly and sponge were stuck to the top of his head like a fez.

Did they all laugh? What do you think? They nearly fell off their chairs, doubled up with tears running down their faces. Mam was still chuckling to herself as she carried on cleaning the next morning.

After breakfast they all sat together and finished opening their gifts. The boys had been given snowboards, all with the same special fin design at the back. The sisters also had hats with torches on the front. Mam had a beautiful dress and some lovely jewellery. Jack had new gauntlet gloves and goggles for his bike. While Bob had been given a torch that lit up for miles ahead at night. Buster had a walkie-talkie set, which made him very happy, and Bumble had a compass and bobble hat. Tiff and Joey had a games compendium, a magic light show, and a small snooker table.

The girls couldn't wait to go outside to try out their new skis with their brothers, but first they all had to clear up the paper, tidy their rooms and eat their breakfast.

"Dinner will be at 1.30 sharp, so don't be late," their mother called after them as they skipped down the hall, with their skis and snowboards under their arms.

"Ok Mum," they replied.

As they opened the door the cold air nearly took their breath away. They could hear the church bells ring out in the distance, but they sounded muffled, maybe because of the snow, which was a good half metre deep. Some of the snow drifts were even bigger, like big frozen waves on a rough sea. The two snowmen had grown with the snow overnight and now looked as though they were wearing top hats. As they passed under the snowmen's outstretched arms, the children saluted them again.

The igloo had grown, too, and instead of being round it was now oval-shaped. Looking at it they noticed an orange glow inside and after further investigation found it to be Bob, trying out his new torch.

"Let's put on our skis and try them out." Said Lulu, but just as she said this, the boys went zooming overhead towards the snowdrifts. They had already learnt how to fly their snowboards. The girls weren't as rash as the boys so they started by practising flying just above the ground. They had been skiing since they were young but flying skis took a bit of getting used to. After about ten minutes of flying carefully, they decided to see what else the skis could do.

"These are the best ones we've ever had Shells," shouted Lulu, her voice trailing off into the wind.

"I know. Our old plain wooden ones were fine, but these are covered with a plastic coating and I love the red, white and blue colours. They look so cool," she grinned.

The boys had stopped and had got into position on top of a drift to have another go, looking at each other with excitement, they were ready to fly again, the girls tapped the skis with their poles and WHOOSH, they were flying into the air. The boys tapped their boards and they went up like rockets.

"WOOOOOW." Shells cried. "This is fan-tas-tic!"

They flew around, skimming the top of the leafless trees, whizzing over the half-buried hedges and doing big circles around each other.

"Wheeeeeh," Lulu screeched, "this is the best ever," laughing out loud.

The boys were more reckless than the girls, and started flying just above the frozen river, dodging the reeds and bullrushes that were poking their heads through the ice. Zooooom. As they went under the bridge, they screamed a "Yee-hah," to make an echo as they went.

After a while they heard the faint sound of a whistle being blown. "Mum's calling," shouted Joey. "It must be dinner time already, I wondered why I'm so famished."

They both turned around and began flying back towards the steeple.

They hadn't realised how far they had gone and it took them a long time to get back to the igloo. Unluckily for hr Lulu came in a bit too fast on her descent, tipping up as she landed, and went headfirst into a drift.

Shells came down behind her, just missing the snowmen. The boys landed right next to each other, sliding, spraying snow everywhere and only just stopping on the drawbridge.

They were all out of breath but still buzzing with excitement from the flying and zooming about.

"Wow! That was a blast." Joey exclaimed.

"I'm going out again after lunch to see how high I can go," announced Tiff. "I bet I can go higher than you" he said, looking at Joey.

"You two, you're always trying out out-do each other, said Shells rolling her eyes skywards.

Chapter Twelve

Jack brought in the roasted goose on a big silver tray, and presented it at the table. They all clapped as he positioned it in just the right place. The table was full of all the trimmings, roast and mashed potatoes, carrots, peas, cauliflower cheese, Yorkshire puddings, Brussels sprouts, and jug upon jug of steaming gravy.

"You carve then Dad, and the rest of us can help ourselves to vegetables, so tuck in," said Mam, as shed passed out the plates.

Buster and Bumble had two plates each, one for the portion of goose, and one for their vegetables.

"My, you have a huge appetite," laughed Jack as he put another piece of meat on Buster's plate. "Must be all that fresh air and exercise."

The Christmas pudding had the same treatment, being carried shoulder high to the table, and served by Jack.

"Your Mum made this pudding back in September when all the fruit was fresh and sweet," he explained. "It's been steaming away for three hours today to get it just right. Who wants custard?" Everyone put up their hands.

In the hamper there were some Christmas crackers, so Buster decided to maxify one of them. When all the plates had been cleared away he then put it in the centre of the table. It was now huge, covering almost half the surface.

"Right," said Jack. "Three of you go one end and the other four of you the other end and all together – PULL."

They all heaved together, pulling as hard as they could on the cardboard tape inside, and just when they thought they couldn't pull anymore, "CRACK," it went, and split in half, sending them all sprawling across the floor. Out sprang a huge paper crown, a motto and a mirror.

"Brilliant," said Mam. "Just what we wanted, remember when Bob opened that elderberry bubbly last year and the cork flew out, knocking the old mirror off the wall smashing it to a million pieces? Well, this will replace it. I'll put it up over the fireplace and decorate it with some holly and ivy."

Lulu put some music on while Jack added some more logs to the fire. The rest of them relaxed in the easy chairs, after lunch, enjoying the warm glow inside the room and inside their tummies.

It didn't take long before one by one, they had all dropped off for a nap.

After a while, Joey stirred and looked out of the window. He saw it was just turning twilight. There was maybe half an hour before dark. Just enough time to try out the snowboards once again. He nudged Tiff, who was miles away gazing at the Christmas tree.

Joey gestured to him to come over and very quietly they got up and left the room, closing the door very gently behind them. It had stopped snowing now but when they were outside, the wind whipped up the fallen snow and it cut into their faces. "Is this a good idea, Tiff?" asked Joey, looking a bit uneasy.

"Just pull your hat down over your ears and get your scarf to cover your nose and mouth and you'll be fine," he replied.

So off they went. First up was Tiff, with Joey following closely behind, skimming just above the ground to start with. Soon they'd forgotten all about the cold. The torches on the front of their boards lit up the snowscape so brightly they could see for miles. It was wonderful seeing all of the lights on in The Grange and the huge Christmas tree in the middle of the courtyard. They flew past, quite close to the Steeple and glancing quickly through the leaded window they could see most of the others were still fast asleep but Shells and Lulu were sitting in the window seat with their little faces pressed up at the window, watching them. How warm and cosy it looked in there with the fairy lights blinking and the glow from the fire. Icicles sparkled around the outside of the window. Seeing this made them feel the cold again.

Tiff signalled to Joey that he was going to try and do a loop the loop.

"Loop the loop?" Joey shouted back. "You must be joking mate. We've only just learnt how to handle these boards, that's a really tricky move I reckon."

Tiff just shrugged his shoulders and flew over to a snowdrift. He levelled out and then shot straight up and up and up in the air. When he had gone about fifty metres high, he leant back and started to go over in a big arch.

Back inside, the Steeplers were waking up one by one from their after Christmas dinner snooze. Jack stirred and went out of the room to get some more firewood.

Lulu and Shells were watching Joey and Tiff from the living room. Kneeling on the cushion window seat, they watched the boys darting to and fro in the cloudless, early evening sky. They saw them fly right up to the window, hover for a bit and dive down, which made the girls giggled.

It was getting darker now, and soon all Lulu and Shells could see were the torches on the boys' heads and the lights on the front of the boards. They eased forward and pressed their noses against the cold windowpane to get a better look. One pair of lights shot up into the air followed by the other pair. The first pair of lights began to climb into a lovely arch, but as they were coming out of the turn the lights separated and fell down apart from each other. The girls gasped and grabbed each other's hands.

"What is going on out there?" asked Jack, coming back into the room with an armful of wood. The girls were speechless, and Jack was soon beside them at the window.

The other pair of lights joined one light in the sky, which flew off at sharp angle, then the single light dropped into the soft snow by the igloo, which seemed to be lit up inside.

Tiff had been coming out of his loop the loop, when his foot slipped and he fell off the board, plummeting at great speed towards the snow covered ground. The snowboard carried on for a bit longer then also dropped like a stone as well. Luckily, Joey had been hovering and watching, so was able to quickly fly over to Tiff as he was falling helplessly towards the river. Grabbing his outstretched arm he swung him sideways, just centimetres away from a freezing dip. Spinning like a helicopter blade, Tiff landed in a snowdrift, just missing the orange-glowing igloo.

"It looks like somethings gone wrong with the boys." said Jack, but he couldn't see clearly at all, there was only the glow from the igloo. The girls looked at him and Shells said, "I think they've had an accident."
Grabbing his hat and coat he headed for the door.

Earlier, Bob, having decided not to take a nap after lunch, had gone outside to the igloo to cool down a bit after sitting to close to the fire. He thought he'd stay until it got dark enough to try out his new torch. Having tried all the settings, he was just about to crawl out of the tunnel, when he heard two thumps and saw some lights outside. He shone the beam of his torch towards the sound. Through the darkness he could just make out the shape of two legs sticking out of the snowdrift. Standing right next to the legs was Joey. Bob ran towards them following the beam of his torch.

Jack came bounding out of the door shouting. "Christopher, Joseph! What the blazes is going on?" Joey knew they were in trouble because his dad had called them by their proper names.

Sticking his head out of the drift and spitting snow whilst trying to climb out. Tiff said "Sorry Dad, I didn't mean to worry you, but I lost my footing up there when a gust of wind caught me off balance. Luckily, Joey caught my arm and threw me towards the snow drift."

He gave Joey a wink. "Cheers, mate, you just saved my skin," he said.

"That's okay, bruv," Joey replied. "You'd have done the same for me."

With that, they gave each other a big hug and then headed back indoors with the new boards under their arms. Bob scratching his head followed them in to the warm.

Chapter Thirteen

Back in the warmth of the living room, Tiff sat with his feet in a bowl of steaming hot water with a blanket around his shoulders. He was still shivering from his freezing cold snow drift experience.

Meanwhile Joey and his cousins were setting up the walkie-talkie intercoms in different parts of the steeple.

"Where are you now Joey?" Buster was speaking into the microphone on the base station.

"In the cellar," came the faint, crackly reply. "Over."

Buster asked the same question to Bob.

"In the attic and it's bloomin' cold up here, could you hurry up please," Bob retorted.

While this was going on, the two girls were hanging up a sheet as a screen for the showing of the Christmas night premier of "It could only happen to a Steepler", a cine-film diary they had taken throughout the year of all the funny, weird and wacky things that had happened to them all.

Securing the projector on the sideboard and putting drinks and snacks out for everyone, they were nearly ready. Lulu went to the base station of the walkie-talkie set, pressed the button and declared in a posh voice;

"Ladies and gentlemen, the film will be starting in five minutes. Would you all please take your seats. Hot dogs will be on the table in three."

Settling into their seats with drinks and snacks in hand, Shells pressed the start button on the projector and the two reels started moving round and round. They all enjoyed the film. With many 'Oohs' and 'Ahs' and lots of laughing at all the funny things that had happened during the year.

Over in the corner of the room Lulu sat staring out of the window at the dark night outside. She sighed heavily, 'I wish the Snow Circus would come' she said to herself. 'I so want to see the Snow King and Queen'.

When they had all washed up and retired to bed, bidding each other a fond good night, silence fell upon the Steeple.

All the Steeple People were exhausted and fell asleep straightaway. All you could hear was the ticking of the grandfather clock in the hall. Peace had at last fallen on the Steeple.

It must have been midnight when a strange light appeared outside. It shone faintly through the curtains, a mixture of all the colours of the rainbow at the same time. The wind stopped blowing and it became very, very still, but no one stirred, they were all fast asleep.

Chapter Fourteen

The Boxing Day sun shone brilliantly through the crack in the curtains and, outside, what a sight to behold. In the field was a huge castle made of pure ice. The bright sunshine danced on its turrets.

Next to it was a big top with red and white stripes. Behind that was a huge Ferris wheel with open carriages.
Flags and long pennants were fluttering in the breeze.
There were fire pits dotted all around. Snowmen, Snowwomen, Snowdogs and Snowhorses were all doing their work, putting up smaller, brightly coloured tents. Snowponies were pulling different coloured sleighs filled with assorted boxes.

Shells and Lulu dressed and not giving a thought to their breakfast, leapt down the stairs two at a time and were outside as fast as their little legs could carry them. Quickly putting on their skis they started skiing through the snow, zigzagging without any magic, only using their poles. They loved skiing together and were laughing and shrieking as they went. The cold made their cheeks glow bright red between their goggles and scarves. The boys came whooshing overhead, making the girls shriek even louder. Shouting and whooping, they soared over the top of the castle, circling twice so they could get a good look, then landing right in front of the big top, shooting snow everywhere, as you do when you come to a stop at the bottom of a ski slope. It took the girls a few minutes to catch them up, but they didn't mind because they loved seeing the castle looming ever closer, taking in the wonder of it all.

Standing next to each other the girls looked around at this awesome sight. A snowman who was much bigger than them, with a red coat, black top hat, white trousers and black boots walked up to them, took off his hat and very slowly bowed, greeting them with a broad smile.

"Welcome to the greatest snow circus in the world," he boomed. "Are you the Steeple People we've heard so much about?"

"We are," whispered Lulu, looking at Shells and wondering how he knew who they were. "We're so excited that you've been able to come this year, Mr Snowman."

"We're delighted that we've been able to get here young lady. The wind was in the right direction for the first time in years. The last few Christmas's we've been to Norway, Sweden, and Lapland," replied the snowman.

"Oh my. What was Lapland like?" asked Shells. "Did you see Father Christmas?"

"We certainly did, on Christmas morning, just after he'd delivered all the presents. He was in such a good mood. We had a special throne made for him out of ice and sat him between the Snow King and Queen on a big red velvet cushion to keep his bottom warm. Then he watched the show, chuckling and giggling all the time at the antics of the snow clowns and the acrobats, especially the flying trapeze artist, Nina Ryebeana. He had so much fun that day. Once the show had finished, we had a banquet in his honour in the marquee we had specially erected for him. It seated two hundred guests from all over the land. We feasted all night while the jugglers and jesters entertained us. At midnight he jumped into his sleigh and flew out of sight, waving as he went." The snowman grinned at the memory.

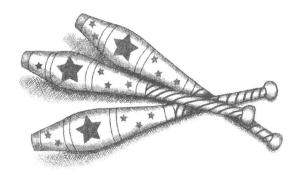

"That must have been brilliant to see," said Joey.

"It certainly was, and our show today will be just as good for you and your friends. When you have finished looking around come to the castle and I'll introduce you to their Royal Highnesses, the King and Queen. I know they can't wait to meet you all." With that the snowman removed his hat again, bowed once more, and walked off into one of the small tents. The children were flabbergasted. Why would the King and Queen want to meet them?

Jack turned up with Mam on the back of his motorbike. Bob, Buster, and Bumble were in the trailer attached to the back. After they had cleared the snow from the doorway, Jack had hooked the trailer to the back of the bike and driven it over the drawbridge, towards he circus, arriving just as the snowman had finished talking to the children.

"He seemed like a nice chap," said Jack getting off the bike. Mam got off the back and the lads fell out of the side of the trailer when Bumble opened the door. They all landed on top of each other in the snow as they rolled out.

"Look at you lot, you're as daft as brushes," laughed Jack.

Lulu and Shells told their parents about the invitation given to them by the Snowman. Jack turned to Mam and looked puzzled.

Other people from the villages nearby were turning up to see the spectacle too. Bladonites, Stonefieldites, Combies and Hanbros were all making their way towards the castle. They came in many different types of transport, mostly horses and sleighs, but some came on snow scooters and others on skis. There were some sledges pulled by dogs and even a rowboat, adapted with runners to go over the snow.

As they moved nearer the castle, Lulu turned to Shells and whispered. "Is it getting darker or is it my eyes?"

"You're right, it is getting darker. Look." Shells pointed to a big black cloud in the sky, moving towards the castle. Everyone was looking at it and everyone was smiling to one another nodding their heads.

"What's going on I wonder?" murmured Bob.

A small snowman standing nearby turned to him and said, in a clear, fresh voice, "They are about to arrive."

"Who's about to arrive?" asked Buster.

The snowman turned to the castle, raised his arm in the air. "The Snow King and Queen, of course."

With that there was the loudest crack of thunder and the brightest flash of lightning they had ever seen. What looked like glitter started falling from the dark grey cloud, descending to the ground at the back of the castle, where it began forming into two human like shapes which then disappeared from view. Everyone stood gaping at each other, their eyes wide open.

"Flippin' heck, did you see that?" exclaimed Buster.

"Of course we saw it, numpty," said Jack raising his eyes to the sky, "Everyone saw it."

Everything went deadly quiet. Then, in the distance, from behind the castle, they could hear a regal fanfare and it got louder and louder. From around the back of the castle came a procession of Snowponies pulling sleighs.

The ponies all had bells on their legs, ribbons in their manes and a long feather at the top of their heads between their ears. All the snowmen in the sleighs wore different coloured coats and hats, and the dogs that ran by their sides wore spotted red handkerchiefs around their necks.

As the procession snaked its way around the front, they could see the last but one carriage was made of gold and inlaid with jewels. Inside were the Snow King and Queen. How magnificent they looked with their tall, gold, glistening, bejewelled crowns on their heads. As they entered the castle through the portcullis everybody clapped and whistled, cheering on the procession.

As it went out of sight Jack suddenly felt a hand on his shoulder and turned round to see a thickset fellow grinning up at him.

"Hello Fizz. How the devil are you, my friend?" asked Jack.

Fizz's grin got broader. "Very well, Jack, very well indeed."

"Have you been blowing up any chimneys recently?"

"Actually before the weather turned I blew up three. Big-un's over Didcot way. My, what a spectacle that was. People even camped out overnight to see that explosion. Magic, it was. Pure magic."

Fizz was a miner by trade or a Fizzler as they were collectively known. The miners all dwelt in the old slate mines in Stonesfield, down in Stocky Bottom. There were a lot of mines there, about fifty of them, where they extracted the stone to make roofing slates. Previous to that they used to mine gold and precious stones.

As Fizz, and his fellow miners, Fidd and Pop, as well as Smokey, their old English sheep dog, continued their pleasantries with Jack and his family, Joey noticed an aeroplane flying towards them, preparing to land. He turned to Tiff and nudged his arm.

"Who's that then, bruv?"

Tiff shrugged his shoulders and looked at his dad to see if he recognised it.

"Oh, that's Captain 'Dodger' Dibbens. He's coming to have a look as well," Jack said, smiling to himself.

As the banana coloured biplane with a red stripe down the side skidded to a halt, Jack cupped his hands to his mouth. "Morning, Captain," he called.

"Morning, Jack," Dodger replied, in his clipped tone. He stepped out of the cockpit and climbed down the ladder. Taking off his goggles and gloves, he walked over to them.

"Saw a lot of flashing lights in the sky last night, so I thought I'd come over and have a gander. My, what a fine sight eh?" Unbuckling his leather helmet and loosening his fur-lined coat, he gave a twist on each end of his waxed handlebar moustache. Extending his arm he shook Jack's hand firmly, "Lovely to see you, old bean."

"And the same to you, Dodger," replied Jack, slapping him on the back and shaking his hand.

The small group had turned their attention back to the circus and Lulu grabbed hold of Shells' hand and squeezed it tightly because never before in her life had she been so excited.

"We're going to see royalty now," she whispered. "The King and Queen of Snowland."

"I know, I can't believe it either," squeaked Shells.

You could almost taste the excitement as one by one the family made their way up a flight of elegant ice-steps.

Chapter Fifteen

Everyone was ushered into a large room where they saw beautiful frozen sculptures. Lining the walls were delicate tapestries depicting great Kings and Queens of times gone by and animals that lived in the wild, stags, bears, wolves and foxes. All kinds of fabulous-looking birds were flying round the vast ceiling. Pictures of landscapes also hung on the walls, and draped round the outside were gold and red silks. Scenes of hunting and battles from long ago were painted on the walls in such a way that they looked just like the hieroglyphics of the pyramids of Egypt.

"Come this way," said their snowman friend, gesturing with his gloved hands towards the big heavy ice doors. "Their

Royal Highnesses are ready to receive you now." He pushed open the two massive doors and led them through to the magnificent Throne Room.

The family looked at each other and smiled with anticipation, as they proceeded to the end of this massive room they could see a raised platform and on it sat two figures, in robes of gold, red, and green. They were wearing beautiful crowns on their heads. Next to them were two Snowlions who also wore matching crowns.

The hall was decorated with dozens of flags hanging down from the ceiling and the walls were hung with more beautiful tapestries. The thrones were changing colour all the time, from yellow to blue to red and green; the colours reflected on the crowns, which gave the effect of glitter balls twinkling on the ice walls and ceiling.

Getting closer, they could see the King and Queen were smiling at them as they stopped at the foot of the steps leading up to the platform. The King stood up, stepped down from his throne, then bending down he beckoned Jack to come to him.

Jack, looking a bit nervous, stepped up onto the platform, he had to crane his neck to look up at the King who was at least three-metres tall. His robes were made of the finest gold cloth and his gloves of pure red velvet. The diamonds in his rings were as large as eggs. Jack didn't know what to do so he gave a polite bow.

"Welcome, my friends, welcome to you all". The King spoke in a deep, rich voice.

"We owe you a great debt for helping us long ago," said the King.

Jack looked puzzled as he glanced at Mam and then the children. In his poshest voice Jack asked, "Pray what debt do you refer to Your Royal Highness?"

"Ah," the King replied, "This is a story that I've related to my loyal subjects on many occasions and now I am ready to tell you. Please make yourselves comfortable on these cushions and I will explain everything." Once they had all sat down, the King began.

"A very long time ago, soon after the Queen and I were married, we were blessed with twins, a girl and a boy. They were the apples of our eyes, but one bitterly cold night as we were travelling back from a royal visit, a terrible snowstorm started raging. The carriage we were in, drawn by six handsome horses, was having a hard time going through the deep snow and freezing wind. All of a sudden there was a lightning flash, followed by a loud clap of thunder. This frightened the horses so much that they reared up, making the carriage almost tip over and shook everyone about. It took quite some time for the horses to calm down enough for us to carry on our journey back to the palace. We were very relieved when we arrived home.

However, when we did, we realised to our utter horror that one of our children was missing. Baby Stephen was no longer in the carriage. Somehow, when the horses had reared up, he must have fallen from his crib and out of the window, which had jarred open when we crashed down into the snow."

The King paused to steady himself at the recollection of the dreadful memory. Once he'd gathered himself he carried on with the story. "We organised a search party and started to retrace our steps back into the night, but it was still another hour's ride to the actual place where the accident happened and the night was deathly cold." He glanced at the Queen and taking her hand he held it tightly.

"The Queen was beside herself with worry, dreading the worst had happened to our poor son. Little did we know, crossing the path of where the accident happened was your grandfather, John Wakefield Steeple."

Lulu and Shells took a sharp intake of breath and Joey and Tiff looked at each other, their mouths wide open.

"John Wakefield Steeple, who, just by chance, was coming home late from

working on the train station roof. By
the light of his lantern he came across a
bundle of cloth lying in the road, half
covered in snow. As he looked down at
it, it moved, and he could hear the faint
cry of a baby. Kneeling down he
carefully opened the folds of the shawl
and found our little baby inside,
embroidered on the shawl was a royal
crest. He gently picked up baby
Stephen, cradled him in his arms and
tucked him inside his jacket, close to his
body for warmth. There was only one
place this baby could have come from,
the Palace, he thought so he began to
make his way in that direction.

It was a very long journey but luckily
he did not have to walk all the way
there. By the time he saw the lights in
the distance from the oncoming search
party, he was exhausted. He had
walked at least two miles through very

deep snow. On meeting the party, he handed over the baby, told them his name, where he came from, a description of how he'd found him, bade them goodnight. Then he turned back into the freezing night and disappeared into the dark and the swirling snow."

The King looked at the Queen and smiled, giving her hand a squeeze.

"The Queen had been inconsolable. She had convinced herself that baby Stephen had already perished in the cold but her tears of sadness changed into tears of joy when he was placed back into her arms. When she was told of the heroic journey John had made to save baby Stephen, she vowed to find him and thank him personally. But alas," the King sighed, "we had to move on, because, as you know, we are at the mercy of the elements."

The King's story was finished, but everyone remained absolutely silent and still.

"So," he continued, "we have been waiting to thank you and your family for a very long time. Please accept this gift from us to you."

The Queen rose from her throne, walked slowly over to a small table on the platform, picked up a tiny casket and handed it gracefully to Jack, who bowed as he held his hand out to receive it.

"Your Highness, I thank you very much," he said, in a hushed voice.

"Open it then, Jack," whispered the King.

Jack gave the casket to Mam and while she held it for him, he slowly unclasped the lid. As it opened, a clear, bright light shone out from inside. It was a brilliant white light and it lit up the whole of the hall. Even the King and Queen had to shield their eyes with their gloved hands.

"Don't worry, it's not that bright all the time," explained the Queen. "It's like that because it hasn't been opened for many years. We've waited a long time to present it to a direct descendent of John. Please accept this gift with our greatest gratitude and love."

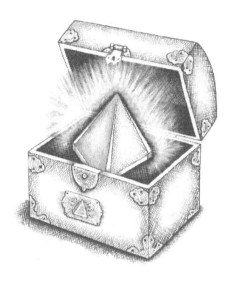

After a few minutes the light slowly began to fade and Jack could now make out the source of the light. It was a diamond. A small, clear, pyramid-shaped prism.

"This diamond has many powers," the Queen said quietly. "Use it carefully for it is very precious and has the power to protect you from harm. It can also heal. But it cannot bring you back to life and cannot be used to do wrong. Take it and cherish it and may it bring you all good luck forever. All you need to do to use its power is say "Rhombus Spectrum" and it will come to your aide, surrounding you in a bubble of white light which cannot be penetrated by anything. If you are hurt it will cover you in an elixir to cure you."

She smiled, bowing to them, and returned to her throne next to the King. The King clapped his hands and in a flash they were all transported to the banqueting hall, with the tables already laden with food.

"How the Dickens did we get here?" asked Bumble. But no one knew the answer.

"It must be magic," Lulu replied, winking at him.

As they tucked into the sumptuous feast, the band played and they all started to tap their feet in time with the music. The jesters and snowmen on stilts performed their act just as they had done for Santa and they all raised their glasses to the King and Queen, then drank the most delicious mead they had ever tasted.

When they were all full, the King clapped his hands again and they were transported to the big top.
"How does he do that?" asked Bumble, "It gets me every time."

First on were the Snowclowns, jumping through flaming hoops, riding upside down on their scooters and jumping from one see-saw to another.
Then the acrobats came on with their death-defying tricks, flips, and stunts. Followed by the flying trapeze act swinging to and fro right at the top of the huge tent all led by Nina Ryebeana. Amazing!

There were Snowleopards and Snowtigers who danced to the music as they walked round, letting people stroke them as they passed by. Next were the Snowhorses and their riders who were throwing sweets to the crowd. Finally, you could hear them before you could see them, trumpeting in the distance, the curtains at the back of the big top rose and walking in a straight line, one behind another, three of the biggest elephants, made from cut ice, came trumpeting into the tent. They were six to seven-metres tall and two-metres wide. They sparkled with every colour in the universe. They swayed from side to side as they walked slowly past with their trunks in the air, trumpeting to everyone. Mounted on their backs were three snowmen, waving flags, and throwing presents for people to catch. A huge glitter-ball hung down from the top of

the roof, with a spotlight trained on it
which sent spikes of colour all around
the inside of the tent. It was fabulous.
Lulu and Shells were totally enchanted
by the spectacle.

Through the sound of the clapping
and whooping, they could just make
out the sound of a small bell ringing
from above. This brought everyone's
attention to the row of heralds with
trumpets in their hands, ready to start

the fanfare. Everybody stopped and turned to look.

The King and Queen stood up from their thrones, walked around the table to the front and in his beautiful clear voice the King said, "Thank you. Thank you all for welcoming us to your homeland. It's been a long time and we wish you all health, wealth, and happiness. Looking at the Steeplers, he said, "Use your diamond wisely as it will bring you goodness and keep you safe. Have a safe journey home and we will see you again when the weather is just right." With that he clapped his hands and they were all transported back outside the big top.

It was nearly midnight. Jack had drunk too much to drive his bike back, so he and Mam got a lift home in the snow-boat. With the diamond safely stowed away in Mam's handbag. The

boys and girls started to head home on
their skis, the lights cutting through the
night. Bumble, Buster, and Bob decided
to walk. It wasn't far anyway and it was
a beautiful night with the moon shining
and the snow twinkling like millions of
diamonds on a huge white sheet
stretched across the floor.

Captain Dibbens clasped hold of the
propeller of the plane and with a sharp
downwards motion he started the
engine. Running round the back, he
pulled out the chocks from the wheels,
jumped onto the wing and slid into the
cockpit. Taxiing along the ice, he took
off waving his hand then flew into the
dark sky. You could see his headlamp
going across the sky like a comet.

Once the Steeplers got home, Jack
put the diamond in the safe in the wall
behind the painting of Mam, and then
they all wished each other good night
and retired to bed after turning out the

lights. Lulu looked out of her window for the last time that night to see the palace. She drew the curtains then got into bed and sighing happily she thought to herself, 'now that was the best Christmas, ever'. With that, she closed her eyes and drifted off to a wonderful deep sleep.

No one stirred until about mid-morning the following day. Lulu and Shells got up first to make breakfast whilst Jack tended to the fire. Again.

Tiff and Joey were playing with their walkie-talkies in various positions in the steeple. You could occasionally hear them laughing as they played tricks on their cousins, who were trying to get some proper work done, like cleaning up the snow and bringing in more firewood.

As for the snow castle - it had gone as quickly as it had come, leaving only ghostly outlines in the snow.

Life became normal again ... or as normal as it can be for a Steepler.

A very Merry Christmas and a happy New Year to you all.

Until the next time.

The Steeple People Song

As the snow swirls around,
Laying deep on the ground,
And the little ones dart to and fro.
The twinkling lights,
through the cold winters nights
Dance playfully on the snow.

Chorus
Oh.. the Steeple People love it
They can't get enough
They play every day and every night
Flying through the air, dashing everywhere.
Oh what a wonderful sight

As the wind starts a blowin'
They all start a-going
They can't get enough of the fun
Flying down the river
Waving to each other
Catching the early morning sun

Repeat Chorus

As the days get shorter
And the nights get longer
With Jack frost starting to bite
When the cold wind blowses
And freezes up your nose's
Then everything turns white

Repeat Chorus

When the pond freezes over
And the ducks can no longer
Go for a swim with their drakes
It's time to get ready
Make yourself steady
and put on your dancing skates

Printed in Great Britain
by Amazon